Perch,
Mrs. Sackets,
and Crow's Nest

Perch,
Mrs. Sackets,
and Crow's Nest

Karen Pavlicin

Alma Little
St Paul, Minnesota

This is a work of fiction. Names, characters, places, and incidents are either products of the author's imagination or, if real, are used fictitiously.

Cover illustration by Martha Doty.
Cover and book design by Andermax Studios.
This book was typeset in Sabon LT and Fontin.

Library of Congress Cataloging-in-Publication Data

Pavlicin, Karen.
  Perch, Mrs. Sackets, and crow's nest / Karen Pavlicin.
    p. cm.
  Summary: Andy does not look forward to spending a summer in West Carthage, New York, but as he does chores for his grandmother and her eccentric neighbor and connects with his mother's childhood friend, John, he begins to accept that faith will help him deal with the changes that life brings, starting with his father's recent death.
  ISBN 978-1-934617-00-7 (hardcover) — ISBN 978-1-934617-01-4 (pbk.)
  [1. Family life—New York (State)—Fiction. 2. Country life—Fiction. 3. Grief—Fiction. 4. Friendship—Fiction. 5. Christian life—Fiction. 6. West Carthage (N.Y.)—Fiction.] I. Title.
  PZ7.P2865Per 2007
  [Fic]—dc22

2007020517

2 4 6 8 10 9 7 5 3 1
Printed in United States of America.

Alma Little is an imprint of Elva Resa Publishing LLC.
http://www.almalittle.com
A portion of all book sales is donated to charity.

For Alexander Maximilian,

who taught me all about summers of courage,

and his PaPop,

who will always be fishing for perch on Red Lake

This is a made up story.

Table of Contents

Summer of Courage

Mom called this my Summer of Courage.

She said that when you need courage the most is when you realize what's happened in your life and you decide to get up the next morning anyway.

That's how it was when my dad died of cancer.

That's how it was on the first day of this summer.

It was the last day of fourth grade, our last game of mud soccer. The last day that Anthony, my best friend since I was three years old, would be in Minnesota. He was on his way to Colorado, where his dad got a new job.

"I'll write," Anthony said.

"Yeah, me too," I said.

We stood on my porch. We high-fived and low-fived one last time. Anthony jumped off the porch and ran next door. When he looked back, I waved then went inside.

Mom was in the kitchen singing. Sometimes her songs remind me of a meadow lark celebrating the sun after a good rain. I listened for a minute and decided this time her voice was a nightingale praying in the dark night.

I wasn't looking forward to this summer. Mom thought we needed a break away from all the stress and changes in our lives. Grandma's idea was to go stay with her for the summer. We said yes, but I wasn't so sure about this plan.

I mean, I liked going to Grandma's. We went every year for a week of vacation and I always had fun. But a whole summer? Grandma lived in the village of West Carthage, in the middle of nowhere in upstate New York. It had to be so boring to live there all the time. In our town just outside Saint Paul there was always something to do.

But I couldn't imagine staying home for the summer either. Not without Anthony.

I plopped down onto the couch, mud and all, and closed my eyes.

Mom and I did our best to keep going, to have courage. We prayed a lot. Sometimes I wondered if God ever listened.

I prayed real hard for my dad to get better, but he died. I prayed that I would win the art contest at school, but I didn't. I prayed that Anthony would be my best friend forever, but that was going to be harder now that we didn't live next door to each other. And I prayed that Mom would learn to cook something besides hot dogs and jelly sandwiches.

Nope, God wasn't listening.

But I prayed anyway.

Mom came in and sat on the edge of the couch. I opened my eyes and looked at her face. She didn't say a word about the mud.

"A little bit of faith, Andy," she whispered.

I closed my eyes again and prayed for God to send me a sign. Any sign he was listening.

He sent me perch, Mrs. Sackets, and crow's nest.

1

Mulch

"Well, if I'd known that, I could have stopped there on the way," Mom grumbled, pulling the truck door shut. "Gray's Flowers doesn't sell mulch. We need to go back to Agway."

Agway was less than a mile back in the direction we'd come, but I could tell Mom was really annoyed that the trip wasn't completely organized and in order.

Back home, we always planned the order of where we had to go. Even though pretty much everything we could possibly need was about a mile or two from our house, it could take a while to drive through traffic and construction.

Grandma's town has only two traffic lights.

Grandma's old farm house sits at the end of a long sidewalk that has weeds growing in its cracks. On one side of her house acres and acres of hills and woods stretch into dairy farms, chicken farms, and maple syrup farms. On the other side lives the village of West Carthage. Across the bridge going over the Black River is Main Street in East Carthage.

We drove past the pharmacy, bank, shoe store, barber shop, and gas station. That's where we found Agway and the mulch.

It was a short drive down Mechanic Street to the Saint James cemetery. Some of the houses along the way looked a hundred years old, with peeling paint and front yards of mostly weeds, dirt patches, and toys. Huge maple trees that looked even older than the houses shaded both sides of the street. We bumped over the railroad tracks and turned into the cemetery.

Mom passed me the hand shovel and pointed to where she wanted the holes. We had picked out yellow and red blanket flowers, small daisies, and black-eyed Susans. I watered each one and gently smoothed the cool mud.

The mud felt good squishing through my fingers. It reminded me of the first time I played mud soccer. I had fallen face down on the wet field and when I tried to get up, my fingers squished through the mud. It felt cool like soft serve. That was the spring after my dad died. Mom gave me a soccer ball and told me to kick it as hard and often as I needed to so all that anger and sadness in my heart had a place to go. Anthony played too. He's the one who helped me get up from the mud that day.

"I miss Anthony," I whispered.

I tossed a few worms on the grass.

Mom nudged me with her shoulder as she spread around the mulch.

I looked at the gravestone.

"I miss Dad," I said.

I wiped my hands on the grass.

"Mom, what are we going to do all summer? I don't have any friends here. What's it going to be like when we go back home?"

Mom set down the bag of mulch and sat back on her heels. "Andy," she said, "Our lives are like novels. The first book didn't end the way we thought it would, but it was still a really good book."

She brushed her hands on her jeans. "Now we begin the second book," she said. "There will be some of the same people in this book, but some new characters, too. We don't know what will happen next or how the story will end up, but what fun would it be to read the last chapter first?"

She picked up a few stray pieces of mulch from the grass.

"The best part of reading a good book," she added, "is seeing the story unfold, page by page, chapter by chapter, even with all its surprises." She leaned over, kissed my forehead, and smiled. "We can still suggest edits to God along the way."

I nudged her back and swallowed hard. Our next book sounded sad and hopeful at the same time.

I looked around the cemetery. An old man reading the newspaper sat in a lawn chair on a grave in the older section. A girl who looked the same age as my babysitter walked to the other side of the cemetery with an American flag.

I used to think cemeteries were kind of creepy. All those dead bodies lying around. But now that

Dad and PaPop are there, it seems kind of peaceful. I wondered who the people were that the man and the girl were visiting. I wondered how they died. Was everyone who came to the cemetery starting a new book in their lives?

A tall man in a Metro Stars shirt walked up the path to our section. "Shhh," he mouthed.

"Good to see you!" he said as he walked up behind Mom. She turned.

"John!" Mom threw her arms around his neck and he swung her around. "My mom said you were hanging around."

2
Wobbly Knees

Floating in the water, I adjusted my grip on the rope handle and put the ski tips up in front of me to try again.

"Keep your arms up straighter!" Dori yelled.

Mike sped up the boat and I started up out of the water. Splash! This time I fell face first and it felt like I swallowed about five pounds of water.

"Are you okay?" Mom yelled. I could only cough so I waved my arm and put my thumb up. This was harder than I thought it would be. Mom and Dori both made it look so easy.

Mom has been friends with Dori since second grade. Dori's husband, Mike, grew up on the Black River. It's not a wide river, but the current is powerful near the bridge. Mom says the James River Company used the river's power for its paper mill until the mill closed about ten years ago, about the same time I was born. The section we were in, a couple miles downriver of the bridge, is calmer and wide enough for water skiing.

I decided to give it one more try. *I can do this.* I repeated the steps to myself: skis straight, arms straight, knees bent. I gave Mike a thumbs up to go.

"Yeah!" They all yelled from the boat. I didn't dare look at them. I just kept focused on the wake in front of me. My knees were wobbling.

"Bend your knees!" Mom yelled.

"I'm up!" I yelled. "I'm up!" I held the rope as straight as I could and stayed right in the wake.

We took a sharp turn around the river bend. "You can do it. Just hang on!" Dori called.

I was outside the wake, skiing along the side. It was way cool and a little scary.

It got easier once I got into the rhythm of the skis bumping across the water. I looked over to the bank. A man was showing a boy how to fish. I wondered if it was his dad. Up the river, two boys were building a tree house with wood. I wondered what Anthony was doing. I hadn't gotten a letter from him yet.

Mike slowed down the boat as we came up to their dock. I tried to balance on the skis as long as I could to come in gracefully.

"Ouch!" My legs spread apart and I landed on my bottom. I didn't know water could hurt like that.

"Nice job!" They all hooted and hollered, standing and clapping from the back of the boat. I put the skis up on the dock and put my thumb up high in the air.

"I did it!" I yelled as loud as I could.

The first week at Grandma's had been a lot like our other summer vacations. A day at Uncle Greg's in Ogdensburg, fishing off the docks and swimming in the Saint Lawrence River. An afternoon at Sackets Harbor on the boat with Great Aunt Martha, getting history lessons about the wind dying down to stop the British ships during the War of 1812, and eating ice cream at Karen's at the Boathouse. Golf with Grandma, swimming in her pool. Relaxing days and awesome food.

But now, there was one big difference: I got up on water skis!

3

Chores

"Well, now, you aren't a very good worker, are you?" Grandma stooped over me with her hands on her hips. Her short, fuzzy blonde hair waved in my face. Her sky blue eyes were larger than quarters staring down at me through her thick glasses. "Lying around on that couch all afternoon. Did the weeding take that much out of ya this morning?"

"Grandma, it's summer vacation. I'll be here all summer. I should spread out the chores a little, don't you think?"

"Ha!" she said, huffing back to the kitchen.

Luke Skywalker was just about to confront Darth Vader when Grandma came storming back in. "You missed half those weeds, Andy Parker!"

"No way, Gram." I tried to make it look like I was stretching so I could see the TV behind her.

"Get your lazy bones out here and see for yourself." Grandma turned off the TV.

We stood over the row of carrots and sure enough if there weren't weeds all around those little fern tops. Huh. How did I miss those?

Grandma walked through the garden and pointed out the weeds I had missed. When she got to the potatoes, she pulled up a weed that was easily two feet high. She looked at me over the top of her glasses, holding out that weed as evidence, and the two of us just burst out laughing.

"No, Grandma," I admitted. "I guess I'm not a very good worker."

John walked up from the back field, his arm muscles bulging under his Life is Good t-shirt as he carried up a fallen tree limb. With his broad shoulders and long strides, he reminded me of a cowboy. Except that his messy brown hair stuck out of his Yankees baseball cap and his tan face smiled like a boy who had just played a joke on someone.

"Weeds sure do grow fast, don't they?" He winked at me.

"Don't you give him any excuses." Grandma pointed her finger at us.

"We'll need the apples picked up so John can mow tomorrow," she added, looking around the property as if she were mentally making a very long to-do list for both of us.

She looked at me thoughtfully and then offered, "I'll pay you five cents a bucket. Only pick up the apples on the ground. Don't pick any from the tree."

That seemed easy enough. John set down the tree limb near a pile of stacked wood and showed me where the buckets were in "the building." That's what Grandma called the old barn down by the garden.

When Grandma told Mom that John was hanging around she really meant that he was staying in her attic in exchange for helping with some projects she needed done. I didn't remember Mom ever talking about him before, which was strange because they seemed like best friends, like me and Anthony.

The apple tree branches twisted and coiled up into a tangle of red and green. The tree was loaded with apples about the size of golf balls. I set the buckets down under the tree and picked up a handful of apples from the ground.

"Gross!" I whined out loud. I looked at the brown mush on my hands. The apples were bruised and rotten. I picked up another by its stem. It had worm holes. Some were as hard as rocks. Others were as soft as applesauce.

"They're not dirty underwear, you know." Grandma marched back down to supervise. "It'll take you all night if you pick them up one at a time."

Her hands were on her hips again. She watched me as I tipped an empty bucket on its side and tried rolling the apples into the bucket with one finger. Grandma scooped up a bunch and tossed them in the bucket.

"You drive a hard bargain," she said, standing up and wiping her hands on her homemade apron. I looked up at her, confused.

"One dollar for each full bucket if you get them all picked up before dinner."

I figured there were probably five buckets worth of apples beneath that tree and worse ways to make five dollars. It was certainly better than the nickel a piece she was going to pay me.

Grandma was already back up to the kitchen door. I called after her, "Do you want me to dump these in the compost?"

"Compost?! Those are my baking apples, Andy!"

4
Red Lake

The light switched on and off, on and off.

"Time to get up," John said in a husky voice.

It was dark, not even a glimmer of morning light outside my windows. The window next to my bed faced east and during other vacations at Grandma's, I had watched a few sunrises over those trees. The sun was sound asleep, which was where I thought I should be, too.

I rolled over and pulled up the sheets. They smelled like sunshine and apples and all that was good in Grandma's yard.

John grabbed my big toe and pulled me sideways off the bed.

"I'm up," I mumbled.

He walked out and left the light off. The switch was by the door, clear across the large room. My bedroom was in an old part of the attic that had been refinished. I bumped my head on the slanted ceiling and tripped over my shoes before reaching the light switch. I decided it was too bright anyway, turned the light off again, and waited a minute for my sleepy eyes to adjust to the dark.

John was well into a bowl of Cheerios when I shuffled into the kitchen. "Tell me again why we are up so early?" I asked.

He slurped the bowl of milk and replied, "That's when the fish bite."

He stuffed two bologna sandwiches, two apples, a Coca-Cola, and a Fruit Juicy Red into a metal

Star Wars lunch box. When it wouldn't close, he put the apples in his jacket pockets.

He had already hitched the boat and trailer. We loaded up the pickup with life jackets, a cooler, and nets.

"We're forgetting something," he said, stretching his back. He looked back in the truck and raised the tip of his ball cap.

"Bait," he said. "Jigs are on the counter, worms are in the refrigerator."

Grandma's refrigerator was the only place I'd ever seen cottage-cheese containers with bait in them. At Christmas time, she had spikes or mousies for ice fishing. "Watch what you're eatin'," she would say. I opened the container to make sure I had the worms.

"How long are you going to stay at Grandma's house?" I asked as we rode along in the dark, our cargo clinking with each bump and pothole in the country roads.

"At least for the summer," John answered. "I'm thinking about building a house up in Champion, out near the Hanson farm. I've been looking at some land out there, maybe build next summer. I figured your grandma could use the help and I need a place to stay until I decide what I'm going to do."

John told me all about his years living in Washington, D.C. He moved there right after college. His mom died a few years ago and he came back to Carthage to bury her next to his dad. "That's when I started thinking about maybe coming back to stay," he said. "I kind of miss small-town life."

He told me all about growing up with Grandma and PaPop being like a second mom and dad to him. "Your mom and I were best friends since about the fifth grade. I lived just around the block, and your Uncle Greg and I played on the same ball teams. I guess since I was always over there, your grandparents figured they might as well feed me and scold me and give me college advice just like the rest of their kids."

As we turned off Route 37 in Theresa, he added, "I fished a lot with your PaPop and Uncle Greg. I never did catch near as many as either of them. I think they practiced on the side when I wasn't around."

We got to Red Lake just as the sun was coming up. Mist rose above the calm water and the air was stuffed with a musky, mildew smell.

John backed the truck down into the boat launch and put the trailer in the water. He threw our gear into the bow, then released the winch and rolled the twenty-foot Lund off the trailer. I held the boat rope while John parked the truck.

I watched John steer the boat away from the reeds as we slowly picked up speed and started skimming toward the center of the lake. He found a spot and turned off the motor to drift a bit. I followed his lead and put a piece of worm on my hook.

I asked a lot of questions, too many I guess. John just looked at me and said, "Are you trying to scare away the fish?" He told me about fishing with PaPop. No one was allowed to talk.

"I didn't understand how the motor running the whole way out to the fishing spot wouldn't scare away the fish, but one of my quiet questions was somehow going to disturb their appetite for breakfast." He laughed. "PaPop sure knew what he was doing though. He's the best fisherman I've ever known."

John patiently took my rod and, without saying a word, reminded me step by step what to do. He didn't say we couldn't talk, but I felt like maybe I had already said too much. I pretended PaPop was with us.

I could hear the line coming off the reel then plop in the water. I'm sure there was wildlife all around us making noise, but all I heard was the reeling in.

"There's one," he whispered. "Here we go." He set the hook with a swift jerk of his wrist. I could hear his sleeve against his wind breaker. Jzz zzzz.

"They're over here. Now, don't cast too close to my line," he said. "Down four." That means count to four so you know how deep to drop your line where the fish are biting. I could see a fish at the surface chasing minnows.

I was in the bow and John was in the back of the boat. It seemed like all he had to do was drop his line and he pulled up a fish every time. I wondered what I was doing wrong, how come he was catching them and I wasn't.

We switched places and then he pulled up two from my spot. It felt like the pressure of a penalty kick in soccer. When I finally got a bite, it was a tiny bluegill that we released.

We broke for an early lunch. I carefully held my sandwich with the plastic wrap so I wouldn't get worm guts on it. The smell of the bologna mixed with the swampy fish gunk under my fingernails. It made me want to throw up, but nothing came up except a big yawn.

Since we weren't exactly fishing, I figured it didn't matter if I scared a few fish. "Uncle Greg said PaPop would fish all day long," I said. "How could you come here all day and be so quiet?"

"It's a good time for thinking," John said. "I do a lot of thinking when I'm fishing."

"What do you think about?"

He thought for a while, drinking his Coca-Cola and looking out over the reeds as though he were searching back in time to remember a good story.

A flock of geese flew overhead, honking. The mist hovered above the lake like a dream, filtering the view of the wooded shoreline.

"I remember one morning," he began. "I came out here with PaPop and the mist was rising just like this morning." John paused, scanned the horizon, then continued. "I had a girl I was interested in. I swear I could smell her perfume in that mist. I thought about her all day. I sorted out my feelings and didn't have anybody to interrupt me."

We finished lunch.

"Who was the girl?" I asked.

"Your mom."

5

Green Beans

My soccer ball knocked over the plant on the kitchen counter. "Ooops. Sorry."

"Andy! Not in the house!" Mom yelled in her annoyed voice. "Find something else to do. Go outside."

"It's so *boring*," I complained. A few weeks at Grandma's and it was getting old. I missed home. I missed all the things to do in Minnesota. I missed the log chute at Mall of America, that feeling when the log goes over the edge and my stomach feels like it's in my throat as the water splashes over me and I fall to the bottom. I missed the IMAX at the Science Museum, that awesome feeling of exploring a coral reef or flying like an eagle through the snow-capped mountains. At Grandma's? I could weed the garden. Fish. Weed the garden. Swim. And there was nobody like Anthony to do it with.

About the most interesting thing in Grandma's ancient farmhouse was the little hole in the floorboard I found in my bedroom. I dropped a marble down and it came out a hole in the kitchen wall. That was good for about thirty minutes of entertainment.

"Intelligent people don't get bored," Grandma said matter-of-factly. "Here, bring these green beans over to Mrs. Sackets."

Mrs. Sackets lived next door, although there's more space in between her house and Grandma's than the length of my entire cul-de-sac back in

Minnesota. Out of pure boredom, I counted my strides. I lost track around one hundred sixty.

I set down the three bags of beans on the porch and rang Mrs. Sackets's doorbell. No answer. I walked around to the back and knocked. I listened for a minute and thought I could hear singing.

"Mrs. Sackets?" I called.

"Shhhhhh," I heard her scold out the screen window of the kitchen. "I'd almost caught it."

"Caught what?" I whispered. She opened the door and waved me in. She pointed over to the big picture window in her dining room. There was a sitting bench with pillows and a book open. But I couldn't see anything else. "What?" I asked again.

"Oh, can't you see it? It's brilliant today," she whispered.

She crouched over and tiptoed quietly as though she were sneaking up on a rabbit or a bird. I didn't see anything. She reached out carefully with her hands cupped together and scooped up the sunshine streaming in the window.

"It's just perfect this time of day. That late afternoon sun makes a halo around everything. I just love to catch some for myself."

Then she whispered like it was a secret: "Sunbeams are messages from heaven, you know."

I stood there quietly for a minute, not sure if catching sunbeams required the same silence and concentration as PaPop's fishing. Finally, I whispered, "I brought you some beans."

She looked up from her window seat. Sheer white curtains draped gracefully on either side. Her face looked dreamy like she had just woken up from a nap. The afternoon sun made a halo all around her hair. She looked like an angel.

"Oh, I love your grandma's green beans!" Mrs.

Sackets jumped up and clapped. "I'll take three pounds, please. How much will that be?"

"Well, there's no charge. Grandma said to just bring 'em over to you. I have three bags."

She handed me a quarter—"for you, it's a Texas, hard to come by up here"—and a piece of paper with the words *Happy was a cat* written at the top. "Give that to your mom," she said. "And those beans can go right here in the sink. I'll be eating those for supper tonight."

She winked and went back to the window, bending over and looking outside as if inspecting the quality of the afternoon sun as it lit up the barn and the garden fence. I brought in her beans and went back to Grandma's.

Mom was standing on the porch waiting when I walked up. She had a pen in her hand and reached out for the paper. Giggling, she wrote *whose orange fur smelled* beneath the first line. She handed it back to me and said, "Please bring this to Mrs. Sackets tomorrow."

6
God

I picked up the book on Mom's bed stand and opened to the page she had bookmarked. I have a habit of doing that—reading pages of her books. I read the section labeled "how to find peace in your life by making quiet time to reflect."

Mom always says, "Andy, you need to learn how to slow down and relax." To be honest, she isn't the best example. Maybe that's why she was reading the book.

The book said a long walk in the woods is a perfect way to listen to God.

I walked through the kitchen. "Going for a walk in the woods," I announced.

Mom and Grandma looked at me and smiled. I could tell Mom wanted to rattle off a list of safety rules but Grandma had her hand on Mom's arm and she just said, "Have fun."

Grandma's trying to help Mom fix what she calls CWS—constant worry syndrome. She said it's a common illness of overprotective mothers. Doesn't matter if there's a good reason for CWS or not, "a kid's gotta be a kid," Grandma says.

I walked past the garden and over the fence to the old railway bed. Wild raspberry bushes grew along one side. The tracks curved into thick birch and ash. Pale blue peeked through the tree tops. I felt dizzy looking up into the highest branches, mesmerized by the swaying leaves of the tall, tall trees. For a moment, I felt so small in the world.

I could hear lots of different birds singing and cawing, and crickets and frogs from the nearby creek. A red cardinal hopped down a few branches to check me out.

I started to think about what I wanted to say to God. I hadn't read enough in the book to learn how you were supposed to hear God on this walk.

A squirrel ran across a tree branch and jumped to the next one. Something rustled under a bush but I couldn't see what it was. A rabbit maybe? A woodchuck? A few minutes later, a mama skunk waddled across the path with two babies at her heels. I stayed out of their way.

It was peaceful, kind of like being out on the lake with John. I walked slowly, trying to decide what to talk to God about.

I couldn't stop thinking about what John had said on the boat. I wondered if he still felt that way about Mom and if she even knew about it. She called him Brother John.

I had overheard them talking on the porch. John asked Mom why she didn't move back to Carthage.

"You can't go backward in life," she said. "Besides, the Twin Cities offer so much for both of us. There are so many publishing contacts there for me. And Andy has a great school. He loves the soccer program. There are camps of every sort—sports, theater, art, whatever he might be interested in. So many opportunities."

"And no family."

"We come to visit often," Mom said, defending us.

"You can create opportunities here. They don't have to be handed to you."

After a while, Mom admitted that right after Dad died we stayed in Minnesota because it was easier not to leave. It was overwhelming to think about going through all our stuff and moving.

"I don't know if I have the energy to start over again," Mom said. "And I just want to do what's best for Andy."

I thought about that all night. Mom and Dad moved to Minnesota for Dad's job before I was born. They liked it so they stayed. It's the only place I've ever lived. I like my school and my soccer team. I like going to camp and to the Mall of America. Did Mom really want to stay in Minnesota or did she want to move to Carthage or somewhere else? If we moved, would we bring all of our stuff with us? Dad's ties are still hanging in Mom's bedroom. Would she bring those? And what about the poster Mom made me for my room at home? It's a collage of photos of my dad. Each night, I look at the pictures and sometimes I ask her to tell me a story about one of them. What if Anthony came back to visit and I wasn't there? What would Dad think about us leaving our house?

I picked a couple raspberries and popped them in my mouth. They were warm and perfectly ripe. I pushed them to the roof of my mouth with my tongue, squished out the sweet berry juice, and swallowed without getting the seeds in my teeth. Yum.

A couple mosquitoes started buzzing in my ear. In Minnesota, the mosquitoes are so big we joke that they're our state bird. You would think that having grown up there I would remember to use bug repellant. I wondered if that was one of the things Mom wanted to remind me of before Grandma rescued her from CWS. I took off my baseball hat and swatted at them. The urge to scratch started to spread and before I knew it, I itched all over my body. I couldn't tell if it was sweat or the breeze on my leg hairs or actual mosquitoes or deer flies trying to bite me. All of a sudden, they were everywhere. So much for my quiet talk with God.

I ran as fast as I could back up the tracks and into the back field, swatting all around me with my hat and hands.

"Aauugghh!" I yelled in frustration.

I looked up over the hill and saw Mrs. Sackets waving from her flower garden. Her straw hat shaded her face. Her flowered dress swayed in the breeze, keeping time with her zinnias and gladiolas. "Wonderful dance, Andy! Next time I shall join you."

7

Apples

"No, really," Great Aunt Martha explained. "If you put a drop of olive oil in your ear, it makes you hear better."

Great Aunt Claire said, "I read about this product called Debrox and I'm going to give it a try."

"Desonex?" Great Aunt Martha asked.

"No, that's for your feet." Grandma laughed. "I tell you I'm the only one of ya who can hear straight."

Grandma's sisters, Martha and Claire, had come up from Syracuse for her birthday.

"So do you think that will be us in twenty-five years?" Mom joked with her sisters, Emily and Laura. They were crying they were laughing so hard at the conversation.

We were all sitting on the porch, cutting up rotten apples. I had fetched five more buckets full.

"Grandma?" I asked. "Why don't you just pick the good apples from the tree instead of cutting up these rotten ones?"

Everyone stared at me like it was the dumbest question ever asked.

"These are baking apples, Andy," she said. "There's lots of good apple in that bucket and when it's all baked up, you don't know what the apple looked like when it started out."

I looked at my bucket of tiny, hard apples full of bruises and worm holes. Two large paper bags overflowed with the skins and rotten apple pieces. After an hour of all of us cutting, there was barely half a pan full of good apple pieces for baking.

I still didn't get it. It seemed like a whole lot of work for just a few apples.

John got up to get another bag for the compost. He leaned over and whispered in my ear, "It's not about the apples, sport."

I looked at Mom. She was holding her side as she laughed. Grandma and all the aunts and sisters and cousins were telling old stories, poking fun at new ideas, and leaning and elbowing and laughing, all while paring their rotten apples and saving the sliver of any good they found.

8

Poetry

"Mom?"

"Yes?"

"Why are you scratching my head?"

She looked at me and laughed. I guess she didn't realize she was doing it. She had taken me up to Chang's Barber Shop. It was the old-fashioned kind of shop, with the spinning candy stripe outside and the big red barber chairs. When I said "short," Chang asked me if I wanted a high-and-tight. He was used to cutting the Fort Drum soldiers' hair that way. Mom explained that a high-and-tight is a shave up the sides and back with about an inch of hair left on top.

"Whoa, not that short!" I told Chang. I've always liked my hair long. I keep it above my ears but kinda floppy on top. Mom suggested I try a short cut this summer. I told Chang "a boy cut, but not like a soldier." He did a good job.

We were sitting on the pool deck relaxing after a good game of water volleyball. Mom played volleyball in college. I picked her for my team. We beat the pants off my cousins. I suppose it was a little unfair that Uncle Greg was holding baby Sam in one arm and big sister Annie in the other. It made for interesting blocks.

Uncle Greg went inside to put Sam down for a nap. It didn't sound like he was having much luck.

Mom finally answered my question. "Your dad always wore a high-and-tight in the Marine Corps.

He liked to have his head scratched. I had forgotten all about that until just now. Sorry about that." She laughed again.

Mom does that. Remembers things. Tells me stories about my dad.

"So what's the deal with the poetry?" I asked.

Mom and Mrs. Sackets had gone back and forth with that silly cat paper until there was actually a pretty funny poem written on it.

"I used to go to Mrs. Sackets's house every Tuesday after school," she said. "I loved to look through her bookcase. She has some magnificent books. Shakespeare printings from the 1800s, biographies, books about magic. Anything you can imagine, it's there.

"One day I noticed a small book of poetry by Genevieve Sackets. We spent that whole afternoon talking about poetry."

"You write poetry, too," I said. "Did Mrs. Sackets teach you?"

"Mrs. Sackets taught me the most important part, Andy." Mom smiled and looked me in the eyes. "She taught me that poetry, in any form, is simply the story we find in our heart. Most people don't actually listen to the stories in their hearts. If they did, they would hear poetry singing."

Mom talked about how nervous she was the first time Mrs. Sackets asked her to write a poem from her heart. "Mrs. Sackets has a sixth sense," she explained. "I was sure she could hear my heart, even if I couldn't.

"So to help me the first time, we wrote a poem together, one line at a time. The next time, we wrote a poem with each of us writing an alternating line. After a while, we seemed to know what the other might want to say and we were able to lead each other in the poems." Mom chuckled and recited a verse of a poem that was one of their worst.

"Mrs. Sackets said it was the north wind to blame." She laughed again.

Mom told me about the first poem she wrote by herself, during her first year away at college, just before she met my dad. She added a line each time she wrote a letter to Mrs. Sackets. "But she kept sending it back without adding anything to it. She just kept saying 'Listen to the story in your heart.'"

Mom smiled. "When I thought I was done with it, Mrs. Sackets added a line about Orion's Belt and decided the poem should be named March 11 because March is when we see Orion's Belt here and 11 was always my special number."

"Was the poem about stars?" I asked. I've always been interested in the constellations. On a clear night, I look for my dad's star.

"No, it's about remembering, I guess. I was thinking of Mrs. Sackets when I wrote it." She looked out across the field. "But if you asked her, she would tell you it was about John."

9
Chickadee

Sunlight tapped on my face, reaching in from the eastern window to my pillow. A finch warbled near the open window above my head. Other birds answered. A robin. Maybe a cardinal. I rolled over and listened, trying to hear each song and what kind of bird was singing.

In the middle of the morning music, I thought I heard Mom laughing. She hardly ever gets up early. I shuffled downstairs and into the kitchen. Empty. Through the screen door to the porch, I heard her laugh again.

"Mom?"

"Good morning, sweetie," she said. "We'll be back soon. We're just going for a run."

John stood waiting for Mom to finish tying her sneakers. "You know, they're looking for a new volleyball coach at the high school," he said.

Mom stood up and reached for the door.

"Wait!" I yelled.

I ran to her and hugged her tight. I hate it when she goes somewhere without me. It's my own version of CWS. Every time she leaves, it feels like my heart stops for just a moment. I can't breathe, like I just walked out into the cold, dry air of a minus-twenty-degree winter day. I think I'm afraid one day she'll leave and not come back. Just like my dad. Just like Anthony.

She hugged me tight and kissed the top of my head. "I'll be back soon," she whispered.

* * *

Mrs. Sackets looked toward the woods. "There's that chickadee again," she said. She pointed to a tree branch over the gate and handed me the binoculars.

A black-capped chickadee hung upside down feeding on insects. He swung around the branch and looked my way. *Chickadee-dee-dee* he called.

I turned the page of Mrs. Sackets's bird-watching book. "It says that chickadees are known for their courage. Why is that?" I asked.

"Just watch that cheery fellow," she said. "Courage is not always about strength or bravery. Each day, chickadees go about doing what they need to do to survive. They adapt to their surroundings, especially in the winter. They have incredible memories. They know exactly in which cranny of which tree they hid their food. And when things don't go right, they just pick up and start over. They trust that if they fall, their wings will carry them home safely."

Chickadee-dee-dee.

10

Sweeper

"Hey, City Boy!" The boy playing center half-back finally kicked me the ball, and I took off down the field.

"Oh yah!" I yelled as I scored another goal. That made four for the day. It was Friday, the last day of soccer camp.

I didn't exactly make any friends over the week. The better players were upset that I cramped their glory. And a few of the younger players just followed me around asking me to show them more tricks.

In Minnesota, I went to Thunder camp, where professional soccer players taught us neat moves like the Kangaroo, Scissors, and Beckenbauer. I played with older kids from the traveling teams. I wasn't the best player, but my team won a blue ribbon in the Thunder Cup every year I played.

I made sure Mr. Center Half knew about the ribbons.

Mom said camp would give me something fun to do, get me out of the house for a week, but I think she was just tired of yelling at me for kicking my soccer ball in the house. One day I accidentally kicked it onto the kitchen table and it squished her favorite sandwich—cheddar cheese, avocado, mayo, and fresh tomato. She said that was the last straw.

The soccer camp was on the high-school field across from Roggie's chicken farm. It took getting used to the smell. But it felt great to run and kick.

"Hey, Andy, wait up. Nice playing today." Sweeper was the only girl at camp. I think they put her in the sweeper position because they didn't realize how important it was. Those boys all wanted to be forwards so they could score. The halfbacks all hogged the field and the goalie was this big guy who couldn't run very fast. Grandma says their big sport is lacrosse so people don't mind so much if soccer is second best. In fact, most kids don't even start playing until they are in middle school or high school. Since I practically sleep and eat with my soccer ball, I couldn't imagine.

"Hi, Sweeper," I said. I grabbed my water bottle and headed toward the truck where Mom was waiting.

"What are you doing later?" Sweeper ran to catch up with me.

I looked back to see if anyone was watching. Big ol' Goalie Man and Mr. Center Half were staring right at me. I didn't want to get a reputation for hanging out with a girl. *Anthony, where are you when I need you, buddy?*

"I gotta go," I said and ran up to the truck.

11

Polka Dots

"We need rain," John proclaimed, unloading an armful of cucumbers and summer squash. It had been unusually hot, in the nineties, all week. The garden was parched. The grass was turning brown. Since Grandma doesn't have lawn sprinklers or air conditioning, we spent most of the week swimming in the pool or sitting in front of fans.

Grandma sat at the kitchen table drinking a cup of coffee. No matter how hot it gets, she has to have her coffee. She pushed away the cup and called out, "Pool time!" Obediently, we all ran to get our suits.

On my way up the pool ladder, I looked over to see Mrs. Sackets fanning herself under a shade tree. Mom nodded "go ahead."

"It's a doozy today, eh, Andy?" she asked as I walked up behind her under the tree.

"Yes, ma'am. Would you like to come in the pool with us? We'd love to have you."

"Oh, I don't really swim, Andy," she said politely. Then she turned suddenly, her eyes lit up. "But would you teach me that game that you were playing with John yesterday?"

"Marco Polo?" I asked.

"Yes, yes, that's it," she said. As she ran to her back door she called to me, "Do come in, I'll be just a minute."

It actually felt much cooler inside Mrs. Sackets's house. I wondered why she sat outside.

I looked around the house a little while I waited.

There were watercolor paintings on the walls of the dining room. Bright, soft colors with flowers and late afternoon sunshine. Each one looked just like Mrs. Sackets, if she were a flower or a garden or the late afternoon sun.

I wandered into the den. Three walls had stacks of books on the bookcases. Mom was right—every kind of book I could imagine. The entire Harry Potter series. The Herbie Jones books I loved in first grade. A biography of Abraham Lincoln. It was like standing in a library, but with all your favorite books and people. Any book I looked at was one I thought I might like to read. I made a mental note to ask if I could borrow *How to Build Robots*.

On the wall above a small desk was a framed handwritten poem.

March 11

I have run barefoot in the rain,
counted the stars of Orion's Belt.
I have scratched funny faces
*   on dew-frosted windows,*
carried the sap buckets,
slipping on last November's leaves
*   still buried in mud.*
I have run through the sheets on the line,
got out the old red bike,
*   a rip in the seat, one pedal gone,*
and ridden impulsively to Main Street and back.
This morning
I sat in the tire swing,
skipped stones across the pond,
and thought of you.

"Andy?" Mrs. Sackets called.

I walked back to the kitchen. There stood Mrs. Sackets in a bright yellow swimsuit with big white polka dots and a skirt. She had a floatie tube with a frog's head around her belly. She wore a matching yellow and white polka-dotted hat on her head and yellow sandals on her feet. I picked up her yellow towel from the table and held open the back door.

I laughed out loud as Mrs. Sackets and her frog skipped across the field to Grandma's pool.

12

Rain

"You mean your mom doesn't ever make crow's nest?" John asked. "That's incredible. She used to eat an entire pan of it—for breakfast!"

In self-defense, Mom quickly let everyone know that I preferred my apples fresh, not baked, and she didn't need the extra calories.

John looked at her from head to toe. "Well, there certainly are no extra calories on your body," he told her. Mom blushed.

I leaned over the counter and breathed deep through my nose. I did like my apples fresh, but

Grandma's crow's nest smelled like heaven. I don't know if it was all that work cutting up the apples or if rotten apples really did make better dessert. Grandma clarified that the apples weren't rotten, just bruised. You couldn't tell anyway once they were baked with all that cinnamon and butter and nutmeg. A lightly browned biscuit wove around the top, with apples bubbling through. It did look a bit like a nest.

Mom likes to eat her crow's nest with warm milk on top. I like warm milk.

"Besides," Mom said. She was still defending herself. "I don't have the recipe."

"Oh, you've seen me make this a thousand times and your grandmother before that," Grandma said.

John leaned back in the chair. He seemed to be enjoying this diversion from the chores. He took a long drink of his lemonade and grinned at Mom.

"All the good cooking your mom does, I find it hard to believe you're not an amazing cook."

"Think about it," Mom said. "Have you ever seen anyone else ever cook in this house? And why would we even attempt it when absolutely everything she touches is delicious?"

"I don't know. Just figured you'd pick it up."

Mom poured herself some lemonade and sat down. "Good cooking skills don't pass through genes."

"Oh, come on." John asked me, "You're just kidding about jelly sandwiches and hot dogs all the time, right, sport?"

I smiled. "Mom is actually a pretty good cook. I think she needs more confidence."

"And focus," Grandma added. One time when Grandma had come to visit in Minnesota, Mom tried to make macaroni and cheese.

"It was the kind in the box, you know, with the three steps of instructions on the side of the box." I laughed as I started to tell the story. "She put the bowls of mac-n-cheese on the table and Grandma spooned hers right up. Mom asked how it was and Grandma said, 'So this is Kraft, huh? Tastes a bit bland.' You know that little pack of cheese that comes in the box? She forgot the *cheese* in the mac-n-cheese!"

We all laughed, even Mom.

John just shook his head and smiled at Mom. "Well, maybe some lessons are in order then."

"From you?" Grandma howled.

"Hey, I'm a great cook."

"Yeah, like the time you were going to make your mom's lasagna. Show us all how you could whip up an Italian family secret." Grandma smiled at Mom and said, "He forgot to turn on the oven. Couldn't understand why it was taking so long to cook."

The afternoon slipped away in laughter and lemonade, and it took a roll of thunder for us to notice that the rain had finally come.

John jumped up and looked out back. "Barn's open. Laundry's out. Pool floaties'll blow." He yelled over the storm, rattling off a list that sent us all into appropriate action.

Grandma yelled, "I'll get the windows. Let the laundry go. You'll never get that in time."

We were all out the door in seconds. I thought about the tornadoes in Minnesota and wondered if Grandma's town had the same siren warnings. I looked over to Mrs. Sackets's yard. She was trying to get the sheets off her line and the wind was blowing them into her, almost knocking her over.

"I'm going to go help Mrs. Sackets!" I yelled, the raining coming fast.

Mom yelled, "Andy!" as I ran across the field. I could hear John call after her, "Let him go. He'll be all right."

I caught the sheet edge and pulled it loose from the clothes pins. Mrs. Sackets stood there calmly. "Lovely, isn't it?" she yelled, swinging her arm toward the accelerating black skies like she was showing off a game-show prize.

We took the soaked sheets, all crumpled and dripping, in the back door to her laundry room. "Oh, I almost got them all," she said, disappointed.

"All the sheets?" I asked. You never knew with Mrs. Sackets. She could have been trying to catch the rain or the wind.

She stuffed the wet sheets into the washer spin cycle and gave me a hug.

"Thank you so much for coming to join me in this celebration, Andy."

We toweled off and walked into the family room where she had a TV tray set up by her favorite chair, with playing cards on the corner and two glasses of fresh lemonade.

A roll of thunder, lightning, and the light flickered and went out.

"Oh, splendid!" I heard her giggle.

It took a minute for my eyes to adjust. It was only around four o'clock but the sky was as dark as night. From nowhere, Mrs. Sackets appeared in the door. She was carrying a lantern.

"Solar lantern," she announced. "I've been waiting for a chance to use this." She set the lantern on a second TV tray. Her face beamed. I was sure she had planned this very event, storm and all. She seemed so pleased with herself.

"Cool lantern," I said.

"It's from a group called Fifty Lanterns," she

said proudly. "They take things like solar lanterns and water pumps and give them to people in parts of the world that don't have those things. Did you know that they brought the first lanterns to the widows in Kabul? Up in the hills where there is no electricity. It gets dark early at night and the children have no light to read by. The women need light to make things they can sell and to stay safe."

She talked and talked about photos she had seen of Afghani children and how it is important that we remember people are people, put faces and names to them, not be afraid of becoming their friends. What she said reminded me of Mr. Center Half, Goalie Man, and especially Sweeper.

Mrs. Sackets's face glowed in the lantern light. It was like sitting at a campfire with a storyteller.

"I was so taken by the story of the lanterns," she continued, "that I decided I had to buy one for an Afghani woman and one for myself. I was waiting for the right moment to try it out. I wanted to make sure it was really going to help those women." She paused for a moment, evaluating. "It works nicely, don't you think?"

I agreed.

"Were you expecting someone today?" I asked, looking at the two lemonade glasses.

"Why, of course." She smiled. "Drink your lemonade. And prepare to get your hat handed to you in gin rummy."

13

Angels

It rained hard for three days. I thought I was going to go out of my mind. We played Monopoly three times. Watched four movies. Looked through old photo albums. Grandma was antsy too. None of her projects were getting done.

Mrs. Sackets caught a cold, probably from standing in the rain "celebrating." I called her to make sure she was doing okay.

"Andy," she said. "We are all going to die."

"Excuse me?" I asked. I couldn't tell if she was foretelling the end of the world or what.

"Stop worrying, Andy. It's just a cold. They come and go. Just like people. You never know how long they'll stay or what you'll feel like afterward." Then she added, "I'd love some of your grandma's soup."

At that moment, Grandma had been cutting up vegetables for homemade soup. *How does she know these things?* I wondered.

Grandma talked Mom through the soup-making process despite Mom's objections that we don't ever eat soup. Mom quickly volunteered to deliver it, though. She needed to get out of the house as much as any of us. She brought the soup to Mrs. Sackets at lunchtime.

John and I sat on the front porch alone with our thoughts for what seemed like hours. Finally, the rain stopped.

John picked and strummed softly on his guitar. Water from the gutter dripped like a steady drum beat. Birds began singing. "Kind of reminds me of Mom's songs," I said. "She's wants to make a CD, you know."

John nodded thoughtfully, still strumming. "Is that so?" he said.

The world around us seemed to sigh and take a deep breath. John and I sat there under the spell of the stillness.

Across the lawn, I saw Mom walking back from Mrs. Sackets's house. The late afternoon sun peeked under the dark gray clouds, shimmering on the wet leaves and outlining Mom's silhouette. She was singing. Her voice carried above the birds, above the trees, pushing away the thick air and making room for the sunshine.

* * *

The next afternoon the ground was dry enough to play on the back field. It was still mud soccer, but at least we had a little bit of traction to run. I pushed up against John, poking my foot around his leg. He had a few tricks of his own.

"Andy!" Mrs. Sackets called from the top of the hill. John stopped to look up at her and I rolled the ball away from him. Ha!

Keeping my foot on the ball, I looked too. Who was that with her? The girl kicked a ball down into the field. It had to be fifty yards. Sweeper?

She ran down to her ball and dribbled the few feet over to us.

"Friend of yours?" John asked.

"This is, uh," I started.

"Katie," she finished. Katie held out her hand and shook John's. "Also known as Sweeper." She smiled at me. "Mind if I play?"

"I need to get back to cleaning out that basement," John said. "Flooded a bit after that rain."

Katie tossed her ball aside. "We'll use yours," she said, bending in a ready position with her hands on her knees.

14

Warm Milk

"So, you wanna try skiing again this afternoon, Andy?" Dori asked. "You're getting the hang of it."

"That would be great!" I said as I climbed out of the cab seat of the pickup.

Dori's father, Mr. Hanson, greeted us. "So, Andy, I hear you like warm milk."

"Yes, sir. I do."

He walked me out to the barn and said, "Well, then, have I got a treat for you."

The stale smell of the straw floor hit my nose as we walked inside the two-story barn. Sunlight slipped in through the loosely boarded side walls. Empty milking stations ran along the center. The barn could have held at least fifty cows, but there was just one. A black-and-white dairy cow with a head wider than my shoulders snorted our way.

"Andy," Mr. Hanson said, putting his arm around my shoulders. "Meet Bessie."

"Nice to meet you, Bessie."

Mr. Hanson led Bessie into her stall.

"All you need to do is pump her tail and she'll give you a nice cup of warm milk. Here, I'll set the cup down for you." He put a cup under Bessie's udder.

Now, I was quite sure that you didn't pump a cow's tail to get milk. But Mr. Hanson is a very nice man and he seemed serious. I looked at Bessie and looked at Mr. Hanson.

"Go ahead," he said.

I reached for ol' Bessie's tail, and she swatted me like a fly.

Mr. Hanson roared.

"I knew that," I said. "I just wanted to see what she'd do."

Mr. Hanson pulled over a stool and told me to sit on it. He ran a cloth under the faucet, wrung it, and cleaned the udder.

"Rest your head here on her flank. Just relax and she'll relax," he said. He held my hands. "Put the teat in your palm, like this."

"Now, squeeze the teat at the top with your thumb and forefinger. Continue squeezing each finger around the teat, forcing the milk in a stream."

I squeezed.

"Don't be afraid. You gotta squeeze it." He talked in a soothing voice and rubbed Bessie's belly. "Squeeze 'til all your fingers are around it. Then release. And just keep repeating." He chuckled. "You can sing to her, too. She likes that."

I squeezed and released, squeezed and released. I thought I was getting the hang of it, but there was hardly any milk in the pail.

"Takes an average of 345 squirts from a cow's udder to yield a gallon of milk," he said, answering my thoughts.

"Don't you use machines or something for this?"

"We did with the farm, of course. But I'm retired now. Sold all my cows except Bessie. Just couldn't part with her." He patted her head affectionately. Then he whispered, "Truth is, nobody wants to buy an old cow, but don't tell her that."

Mr. Hanson took a cup and dipped it in the pail. "Warm milk," he announced.

It was smooth and creamy. The best warm milk I'd ever tasted.

"Okay, Dad, we put it behind your bench near the table saw," Dori said, walking up to the pail and dipping a cup for herself. Dori and Mom and I had just finished an early morning of garage sale shopping. Dori found an old oak dresser top for two dollars that was in good condition. I used the five dollars Grandma gave me for picking up the apples to buy a box of old Star Wars trading cards. I found a blue border Luke Skywalker to go with my Series One set. And the Princess Leia Organa sticker is worth two dollars by itself.

Mr. Hanson walked over to the second barn and inspected Dori's dresser top.

"That'll work great on that old chest." He nodded thoughtfully, rubbing his chin.

Mr. Hanson reworks and matches up old pieces of wood furniture and makes like-new furniture. He says he enjoys the challenge of putting together puzzles more than making things from new flat lumber. It makes him feel good to "give new life to broken bits of the past."

I looked around the barn. It was amazing the things he had made and had in progress. My dad liked to make things from wood, too. We still had his tools in our garage. I bet he would be impressed with all of Mr. Hanson's tools and projects.

"I think it's the carburetor," John said as he walked out from behind an old tractor, wiping his hands on a towel.

"I thought maybe, too. I'll have Kyle come take a look then." Mr. Hanson walked over to the golf cart. "Let's go, John, I've got some land I want to show you." As they drove off, Dori suggested we walk out to the gazebo and see her mom's flowers. Mom and I followed her through the corn rows and across a grassy field. I almost stepped in cow poop.

"Watch your step," she cautioned.

"You know that clock we have hanging in the den?" Mom asked.

I nodded. It was a small brown clock that looked like it had grass or straw pieces sticking out.

"It came from this field." She pointed to the poop.

"No way," I said.

Dori told me about the "dung clocks" she used to make and sell. She gave one to Mom and Dad for their wedding gift. "First I had to select just the right plop of cow dung," she explained. "One that had a good shape to it. With rubber gloves on, of course, I got down on my hands and knees and scooped up the dung." She showed me how some dung was big enough to go up to her elbows.

"I put it on an old chicken wire rack in the pole barn to air dry for about a month or so," she said, pointing to the pole barn. "When the dung was still moist and just a little mushy, I scooped out a three-inch square from the center of the back to put in the battery case for the clock."

I thought about our clock in the den. "The clock is really light. Is cow dung that light when you first get it?"

Dori smiled. "Nope. It's all heavy and gushy and gross. When it dries, it's as light as a Frisbee." She added, "And it smells a whole lot different too once it's dry."

She went on with details about mixing and brushing on the epoxy and after a day or so, adding a second coat to make it shine. Then she drilled a hole in the center for the stem of the clock and screwed on the face. Mr. Hanson bought battery-operated clock kits from a catalog.

"Does it always take a month to dry?" I asked.

We didn't have a month left at Grandma's. According to Mrs. Sackets's book on robots, one of the first steps is to figure out what shape you want for your robot, the style of head and body, and what functions it will have. I wanted mine to be an automatic robot that sensed where it was and made a noise or movement when it got close to something. How cool would it be to have a cow dung head. Ha! I laughed out loud.

"I'm not sure I want to know why you are thinking about drying out cow dung." Mom raised one eyebrow. I just smirked and shrugged my shoulders.

Dori led us over to a cobblestone path.

The three of us stepped up into the gazebo and looked out. It was like a picture out of Grandma's *Better Homes and Gardens* magazine. Stone paths. Flowers of all colors and shapes. Bird houses. A sitting bench. I decided this must be where Mrs.

Hanson came to talk to God. I couldn't imagine a prettier place.

And with all that warm milk in my belly, that bench looked like a good place for a morning nap.

15

Hillbilly Heaven

Mom put a stack of pancakes in front of me. I forgot. That's another thing she can cook: blueberry pancakes. I reached for the syrup that Grandma and I had picked up from Rohr's farm on the way home from blueberry picking.

John sauntered in.

"You won't believe where this clown took me last night," Mom said, hands on her hips and chest out big. "He told me to dress my best for a big night of dancing."

"You should have seen her face when we turned

onto old Stoddard Road and pulled into Hillbilly Heaven!" John howled. "The Buckshaw Band was playing. Man, were the square dancers out in full swing last night."

Mom told us about Joe, the bartender, who said he had a cousin who lived in Minneapolis. "He was shocked I didn't know him," she said.

She flipped some pancakes and John took her hand, spatula and all, as they twirled around and showed us a cool dance move they learned. With their heads so close together, I noticed that Mom's brown hair matched John's. Then John took the spatula and sang an awful rendition of the band's signature song, "My Cow, My Love."

"Good thing you aren't singing on Mom's CD," I said. "You'd better stick to guitar!"

As Mom and John told us all about their night out, I wished I could have been there, watching Mom dance, seeing her eyes light up. For a moment she seemed the happiest person in the world.

At the same time, there was a knot in my stomach, and I was pretty sure it wasn't from the ten pancakes I'd just finished.

That's when I first realized that Mom wasn't calling him Brother John anymore.

16

Friendship

"Friendship," Mrs. Sackets pondered from her tree swing, "grows and changes over time. Sometimes it turns into fond memories, sometimes a special kind of love. In the end, we're always given something in one friendship that we can take with us to another."

"But I miss him so much," I complained. "Anthony and I did everything together." I sat down in front of her on the grass.

She smiled a knowing smile. "So you like hanging out with Katie, eh?"

"She's a *girl*."

"A very cool one."

"Yeah, I guess so." I shrugged.

"One friend doesn't replace another," Mrs. Sackets went on. "And loving someone new doesn't take away any of the love we feel for someone else."

Grass stuck to my sweaty legs. I picked through the clover looking for a four-leaf stem.

"Why do you think Mom and John never got together? You know, I mean married," I asked.

"God needed a plan to bring you into the world," she said. "Your mom fell in love with your dad. Everyone loved your dad. We all love John, too."

She sat down on the grass next to me. "John has always loved your mom, Andy. And because he loves her, he wants her to be happy. Marrying your dad made her happy. I think your mom left town to see what else the world had to offer. John left because he couldn't be here without your mom. I think he came back hoping that someday your mom would come back, too."

"Do you think my mom loves John?"

"Well, Andy, I don't think that's a question for me to answer." She searched through the clover with me for a while. I was just about to get up and stretch when she handed me a four-leaf and looked up at the sun. "I believe it's okay for you to go home now," she said. Mrs. Sackets never wears a watch. She just knows what time of day it is by the sun or what she calls her internal clock. She says you can plan just about anything around meal times and bed time, and when you live the same schedule every day, your body tells you when it's time to eat and sleep.

I helped her up and thanked her for the chat. As I strolled back to Grandma's, I wondered where Mom was. She had been gone all morning. I couldn't get John to tell me anything. "Oh, it'll be a nice surprise, champ," was all he would say.

I walked into the kitchen and poured myself some lemonade. Grandma was on the phone. "Yes, just a minute." She handed it to me.

"Hello?"

"Hi, Andy? It's Anthony."

"Hi!" I couldn't think of everything I wanted to say to him, especially with Grandma standing there watching me. She had a funny look on her face.

"You know that creek you were telling me about?" he asked. "Well, I was wondering if you could show it to me."

"Huh?"

The back door opened and there stood Anthony with the cell phone up to his ear. Mom was right behind him, smiling. She said, "I went to the airport this morning and look who was waiting there."

* * *

"Stay out of the water!" Mom called after us.

Anthony and I ran to the fence and then over to the tracks.

"It's behind here," I pointed.

We pushed away the branches and climbed over a big log. The creek ran along part of the railway bed and was full of frogs. Anthony and I used to love to hang out by Wilmes Lake at home and catch frogs. It was really cool to watch them, but Mom always made us let them go.

"Look at that!" I whispered. It was a little turtle. Painted turtle, maybe? I memorized the coloring so I could look it up later.

Anthony reached over and picked it up. "Cool." Its underbelly was outlined in orange with stripes along its neck and feet. "I only see one," he said. I knew he was hoping for a good turtle race.

"The water's high," I said. "We've had a lot of rain. Maybe there's another one swimming over here." A deep pool had collected by the log bridge that Katie and I had made.

We spent the afternoon exploring. Just like old times. I couldn't believe we were together.

"I'm hot. Let's go for a swim," I suggested. I meant in Grandma's pool, but Anthony had a different idea. He was already taking off his socks and sneakers.

"Last one in's a rotten egg!" he yelled and ran over to the big log. "Cannon ball!" he called out and splashed into the pool of water.

* * *

"Thought I told you not to go in the water." Mom looked at me with her disappointed look.

"We fell in," I lied.

"And had time to take your shoes off first?"

"Sorry, Mrs. P, but it was so hot," Anthony said. I shook my head at him so he wouldn't go on. It was better to just drop it.

Too late. "Anthony," Mom started. "You can get sick from that water. Or cut yourself on the brush. The water's muddy and not that deep and it's hard to see what's down in there."

Grandma rolled her eyes. "CWS," she mouthed. I tried not to laugh.

"Katie called," Grandma announced. "She's challenged you both to a soccer game this evening."

"Who's Katie?" Anthony asked.

17

The Club House

"Gin." Finally, I won a hand.

"Let's play poker," Katie offered.

"I'm in," Anthony said.

I reached for the bag of pretzels Mrs. Sackets had left for us. I ate a handful and then spread some on the table for poker chips.

It was raining again so we decided to hang out in Mrs. Sackets's barn. She had a room off to the side with a separate door. Earlier in the summer, she had asked me to help her clean out the cob webs and wash the windows.

"This was your Uncle Greg's club house," she explained. "He and John and all their buddies would come here on Saturday mornings for their secret boys' club meetings."

She chuckled. "They used to have a sign on the door that said, 'no girls allowed.' That is, until John took a liking to your mom.

"They were best of friends. Couldn't separate them," she went on. "The only time she wasn't with him was sometimes when the boys went fishing and when they came to these secret meetings.

"Well," she laughed, "one day your mom came over here and looked at that sign and said, 'Mrs. Sackets, I believe you are discriminating.' I tried to talk her out of it, but she went in anyway. She did everything else with those boys—sports, exploring the creek—so she thought she ought to be in on these meetings, too."

I had to wait for Mrs. Sackets to stop laughing so she could keep telling the story.

"Well, those boys were running around in their underwear, playing some kind of superheroes. You should've seen the look on their faces when your mom walked in."

"What did she do?"

"She turned right back around, walked out, and closed the door. She took that sign off the door and said, 'I doubt I'll be back, but you should keep the option open anyway.'"

Mrs. Sackets said my mom never did have an interest in coming back. But since then, it's just been "The Club House." Boys and girls welcome.

I looked around the club house trying to imagine John and Uncle Greg in their underwear with a bunch of superhero boys. I decided this little room must have changed a bit since then.

The club house walls were painted sunshine yellow. Blue polka-dotted curtains hung on either side of the small window that looked out over Mrs. Sackets's flower garden, the back field, and woods. We sat on old wooden crates around a large empty cable spool turned on its end.

A small green-flowered couch took up the entire wall opposite the door. Against the next wall, an old trunk with a curved top sat under the window. Behind me was a bookshelf with cubbies, filled with pretty flower pots, paint brushes, paints, and board games. In the corner by the door were a few started paintings: watercolors and sketches of Mrs. Sackets's tree swing and flower garden. Turns out she painted those watercolors hanging in her dining room.

Mrs. Sackets said maybe painting is my poetry. I told her about the art contest at school. She asked if I wanted to start with a painting of the creek or maybe of the Rocky Mountains where Anthony lives now. I decided I wanted to paint a man and a boy fishing for perch. "The boy catches the perch," I told her. "It's for John for his new house, so he'll always remember our summer together."

So far, the painting was just the water. I still had a lot to learn and not a lot of time to finish it before we headed home.

Anthony and Katie got along famously. He asked me why I didn't write about her and I just shrugged.

"You know," he said. "I'm making a couple new friends in Colorado, too. It's okay. You'll always be my best friend."

I thought about what Mrs. Sackets said: "Friends grow and change. One friendship gives us love for another."

"Hey, it stopped raining." Katie put her face up to the window and looked over to the field. "Mud soccer, anyone? I haven't shown Anthony my *real* sweeper kick yet."

* * *

"How do you know which one is your dad's star?" Anthony asked me. In Minnesota, we always looked directly over my house. Mom had pointed out a new bright star about a week after my dad died and she told me, "It's a sign he's arrived safely in heaven."

In Grandma's backyard, millions of bright stars twinkled in the black. Anthony, Katie, and I gazed from our beach towels on the pool deck. The sky went on and on forever in every direction. Frogs and crickets and a lonely coyote filled the still night air with their noise, and yet it was eerily quiet.

"It doesn't matter which one it is," Katie said. "Once the stars are up there, everyone can share them. They twinkle to keep us all connected. When my dad was in Iraq last year, he told me that every time I looked at a star—any star—it would be shining his love down to me. And then when the stars came out in his half of the world, he would see my love twinkle right back to him. It was still really hard to be apart from him, but the world seemed a little smaller knowing he was only a star away."

I thought about all the people who were apart from someone they love—on earth and in heaven. All those stars above us twinkled little hellos and bright reminders of love.

The world was full of messages. Even the wind had stopped to listen.

18

Perch

The fish weren't biting.

It was a quiet day on the lake. PaPop's friend Norm was in a small boat over at Green Bay. John said PaPop made up all the names of the areas in Red Lake. No map ever named them, so PaPop did. Looked like it was just as slow for Norm.

John was right: fishing was a good time for thinking. The problem was when I really started to think, my chest got all tight and my throat started to hurt.

When Dad first died, Mom kept herself busy with projects. She said, "I'm afraid of what I might say to myself if I actually stop to listen." Now that I had a little time to slow down and think, I was beginning to understand better what she meant.

I watched the ripples around the fishing line. The boat rocked gently back and forth, up and back. The water lapped against the side. Baby Sam would have no trouble napping out here today.

I replayed in my mind everything Anthony and I did together on his visit. I wanted to tuck away each moment, every laugh, like a chickadee getting ready for the winter, so those memories would be there inside my heart anytime I needed them.

Anthony left on Sunday. Before he left, I showed him the crucifix at Grandma's church. He was impressed.

"It looks *real*," he said. Yeah, I didn't tell him I wanted to cry every time I looked at it. I could tell he felt the same though. We both went to a Catholic school, but neither of us had ever seen a crucifix that looked like it had real hands with real nails and real blood. It made you really think about why Jesus had to die like that. Why did anyone have to suffer when they died?

I thought about my dad being sick and dying. It was hard to remember things we did together when he was healthy. I remembered how tired he was. I remembered taking care of him. I remembered that no matter how much I loved him and prayed and wished that he would get better, he just got sicker. For months and months after he died, it seemed like I thought about him every minute of every day, tucking away all the memories I wanted to keep in my heart, but little by little they were fading away.

I thought about how much I missed Anthony already. I thought about what Mrs. Sackets said about friends. Did that work for dads too?

I swallowed hard.

"You okay, champ?" John asked in his quiet voice.

I looked at him.

Maybe it was the stillness of the air, waiting for something to happen. Maybe it was the sleeping fish or the gently rocking boat. Maybe it was John's kind, blue eyes or the way his voice sounded concerned when he asked. I don't know what it was, but suddenly, all those tears I had been choking on, swallowing down, holding back, came like Monday's rain. All at once and heavy.

"I can't r-r-remember my d-dad." I sniffed, trying to hold back the tears.

I looked down and felt like a baby crying like that in front of John. Mom would've rushed right over and put her arms around me. She would've started telling me stories, helping me to remember. Back home, I would've looked at my poster and seen his smile. I would have made myself rummage through the hollows of my heart to remember things we did together.

John just set down his rod and put his hands on his hips, looking out across the lake like he was expecting someone else to come and save me. Finally, he said, "Tell me what you do remember."

I wiped my nose on my sleeve and tried to calm my chest, which was heaving these little chest hiccups. Little scenes of us playing together came to my mind, but I wanted to remember Dad, not just what we did. I looked at my hands and of all things, I said, "He had big hands."

John nodded slowly. "What else?"

"I remember that we laughed, but I don't remember why or what his laugh sounded like."

The boat rocked. The water lapped against the side. The sky started to sprinkle.

I looked down at my feet, then out to the edge of the lake, where John was still searching.

"I remember that I liked to hear his voice reading to me, telling me stories. But I can't remember what it sounded like." I started to cry again.

John reached into his pocket and handed me a handkerchief. The real cloth kind that you wash. Was I supposed to really blow my boogers into it? *Gross*, I thought. And then I laughed.

John smiled. "You can blow all you want. Boogers are just water and dust. No different than washing your fishy clothes," he said.

After a minute, he picked up his rod again and cast his line. "Seems to me," he said, reeling in slowly, "that you remember the most important parts of your dad, the parts that eventually are all anybody remembers."

He set the bail. "If you remember his hands, he

must have held you a lot when you were small. And if you remember laughter, well, then, your dad knew how to enjoy life and you obviously brought him a lot of enjoyment. If he read to you and told you stories, he must have liked spending time with you and I bet together you created some great stories."

He added, "Your dad must love you very much, even now."

He had a bite.

"Well, what do you know. I think the fish are waking up." He pulled up a nice-sized perch.

"Count to six," he said.

I dropped my line and counted to six.

* * *

"Present for ya," John said as he put the cooler beside the kitchen table. Forty-three perch in all. It turned out to be a good fishing day after all.

19

Stories

"Oh, don't paint it all. I only got one can of paint, you know." Grandma was pacing back and forth inspecting the job. "Just cover those bare spots. If it's good enough for government work, it's good enough for me," she said.

Last year, Grandma took the siding that was left over from what had been put on the house about thirty years ago and she put it up on the old barn. Some of the finish had started to peel off.

John didn't tell her that he had already bought more paint and planned to do the job right.

Mom and John were both up on ladders and I took the low panels.

"So tell me more about the CD you want to make," John said.

Mom started talking about what it was like when my dad died. "You know I've been a writer all my life," she said. "But when he died, I had no words. I couldn't even write in a journal."

John stopped painting, watching her. Mom kept painting slowly in a rhythm.

"Then one night I was standing at the stove trying to cook something other than hot dogs for dinner. And I started to sing. I had this song in my head that I had to get out."

As she talked, I could hear the first verse in my head. I've listened to it so many times. Mom recorded it and gave it to all of our family as a gift. It's a blues kind of sound.

Ever since you've been gone,
*   I've been wandering around*
I see you in everything,
*   hear you in every song*
Yet your smell, your touch,
*   flies away with the breeze*
And all that I'm left with is our stories.
Is it the tears in my eyes
*   that make your image blurred?*
Is your star the closest bridge
*   between heaven and earth?*
How can I lay my head in your shoulder
*   and dream about tomorrow?*
How do I celebrate life without you here?

Mom said she called the song "Stories" because
when you celebrate life, you've got stories to tell.
My dad celebrated life.

Mom told John about how she thought the songwriting might be a gift from my dad or the Holy Spirit as a way to help her express her grief. She thought maybe other people might need to hear those words too. So she kept writing.

"I've got about thirty songs now," she said. "I want to make a CD and sell it and give the money to cancer research."

John just kept watching her, listening.

Then he started painting again and said, "Well, I guess we'd better get recording then."

20

Bahama Blue

I sat there looking into the swirl of Bahama Blue, thinking that the red specs reminded me of Mom's freckles.

I hadn't ever thought about gravestones before Dad died. The color choices. What they say.

I sat behind Dad's gravestone, a wide open space to the right and behind me. I could see the flag flying between the spruce trees. Mom picked this spot near the back next to an open field because Dad didn't like crowds. She thought he might like to see the flag, too. Not that he can see anything, but it made her feel better. Our family has a whole bunch of plots beside and behind him. PaPop lies three doors down.

It took Mom a couple years to decide what kind of stone to get. Last summer we came to visit Grandma, and Mom said she just had to get a stone. PaPop had a stone. It wasn't fair to Dad not to have one just because she was indecisive.

She went into the foundry thinking maybe she'd get him his own single stone, in a dark red, his favorite color. But she came out with a double Bahama Blue. Some days it just looks gray. Others it's a really pretty blue swirl with red freckles.

After she picked the stone, she had to decide what it should say. She came here every day looking at the other stones. "Hi, Jane," she'd say, introducing herself to Jane's gravestone, "I'm going to measure your cross."

She walked around for days with a measuring tape and pencil and paper, changing her mind. There was nothing she saw that she liked. One day she brought Aunt Laura down with her to help her with the layout and spacing of the letters. "Let's see how far down the Cerroni family name is from the top of theirs."

She asked me if I had an opinion about any of it. The only thing I wanted was for her to not put her name on the stone. Not yet. It didn't seem right for people to have their names on a gravestone before they die. And I certainly didn't want any reminder that someday we won't be together.

They were set to blast the stone on a Monday morning after she had finally decided. Sunday night, she came again, searching for an example of a small cross to help her feel like her decision would be okay. That's when she found Jane's.

Now that the stone is in place, it seems like it has been here from the beginning. That it's exactly the way it's supposed to be. It has a simple three-inch cross at the top, our family name under that, and my dad's name and his birth dates on one side. I call his death date his second birthday—the day he was born into heaven.

In Minnesota, I talked with my dad's spirit all the time. I never really thought about him being in one place.

On Father's Day and Dad's birthday, Mom and I send up balloons with our own messages written on them. Even though I can talk to Dad anytime I want, Mom says it's always nice to get a special card or message on a special day. We send the balloons one at a time and watch them sail into the sky until we can't see them anymore. She says they know where to go.

All throughout this summer, I visited the cemetery every week. There was something about being near Dad's resting place. I felt like maybe he heard me better. Or maybe I finally figured out a quiet place where I could listen.

I read Dad my letter from Anthony. Anthony asked about Katie. He wanted to know if I could kick that far yet. His new school doesn't have a soccer team, but his mom said he could try out for the traveling team.

At the end of the letter he asked about John and Mom. "He's pretty cool," he wrote. "I hope he marries your mom."

"What do you think, Dad?" I said out loud.

The truth was I really liked John. I knew Mom did too.

I lay down on the grass and picked out shapes in the cloud-filled sky.

Mom drove up the circle. She walked over and lay down beside me. "Any good shapes today?" she asked. I pointed to a bird cloud.

After a few minutes, she asked, "What would you think about moving here?"

I shrugged my shoulders. After a few weeks at Grandma's, I was so bored I couldn't wait to go home. But it was hard to think about saying good-bye to Grandma and Mrs. Sackets and Katie and John. Plus the people I missed most in my life— Dad and Anthony—weren't in Minnesota anymore. I didn't know what it would be like going back there.

We didn't seem to belong anywhere.

Mom rolled up on her elbow and looked at me. "You know I love you and your dad more than anything. I don't know why things have happened this way."

She lay back down and looked at the clouds again. "What do you think about John and me...?" Her voice trailed off.

This wasn't easy for her either.

"I like John," I said. "Maybe he's in our new book."

I smiled and reminded her, "The best part of reading a good book..."

She laughed. "Yes, I know. One page at a time."

I wondered what Dad thought about all this.

We walked around to the front of the grave. I picked up the watering can and high-fived the little wooden Marine that stood tall among the red and yellow flowers.

"I love you, Dad."

21

Sunbeams

Grandma put the potato salad for supper in the refrigerator, poured herself a cup of her after-noon coffee, and opened the newspaper to the crossword puzzle.

"Andy, will you please go in the family room and get my reading glasses?" she asked.

I stopped at the family room doorway. Mom stood at the picture window in a stream of late afternoon sun. Millions of teeny tiny dust particles floated in the soft beams.

"Sunbeams are messages from heaven," Mrs.

Sackets had said. Maybe Dad had something to tell us.

At Mom's side, I cupped my hands and scooped up the warm sunshine.

22

Faith

"Whoo hoo!" John waved a CD in his hand as he came in the back door.

"You got it?" I jumped up from my seat.

John and Mom spent all week at the recording studio in Watertown working on her CD. John called some of the guys he used to play guitar with. He got them together and they laid the tracks for twelve of her best songs.

"Well, let's hear it!" Grandma pulled a CD player off the counter and set it on the kitchen table. Mrs. Sackets, who had come to return Grandma's soup dish, hugged me tight. We all stood there in the kitchen, listening, for forty minutes. Listening to Mom sing about love and death and heaven and new beginnings. The meadow lark, the nightingale, the voice I'd heard so many times had taken flight. Every song was amazing.

The title song was called "Little Bit of Faith."

...You can't keep searching for reasons why
You'll miss what's right in front of your eyes
If you show a little bit of faith, you know,
God will take care of what comes tomorrow.
Just live each moment with a little bit of faith
And when you pray, child, you've got to believe...
With a little bit of faith, and a whole lot of grace
We'll make it through a life full of changes
A little bit of faith, and a whole lot of grace
Have faith, have faith, believe....

The CD ended, and we were all speechless. Mom started to cry. John put his arm around her. Grandma clapped. Mrs. Sackets said it was true poetry.

I suggested we go cut up those apples and make some crow's nest.

"I thought you liked your apples fresh?" John asked.

He reached over and tousled my hair. I hugged them both. *With a little bit of faith, we'll make it through a life full of changes.*

"It's not about the apples," I said.

Recipe for Crow's Nest

When the author was a little girl, her aunts and cousins gathered on her grandmother's porch every summer and cut up apples for her favorite dessert, crow's nest. Just like Andy's grandma, the author's grandma didn't keep recipes. She thinks the recipe goes something like this (give or take a pinch of this or that):

1. Apple Mixture

Fill a large shallow baking pan with the good parts of the apples that fell from your grandma's apple tree (or 8-10 Granny Smith apples will do, peeled and cut into small pieces)

Add 4 pats butter

Sprinkle 2 Tbsp flour (all-purpose or rice flour)

Pour 3/4 cup sugar over apples

(more if apples are sour)

Sprinkle 1-1/2 tsp cinnamon and 1/2 tsp nutmeg

Mix together and let the apple mixture sit while you make the topping.

2. Topping

Mix together

1 Tbsp sugar

3 Tbsp shortening

1 egg

In a separate bowl, mix together

1 cup all-purpose flour (or 1/2 cup rice flour

plus 1/3 cup potato starch flour)

2 tsp baking powder

1/2 tsp baking soda

1/2 tsp salt

Add flour mixture to egg mixture alternately with 1/3 cup milk.

3. Bake

Spread biscuit topping *thinly* over top of apple mixture.

Bake at 375 degrees Fahrenheit uncovered for approximately 40 minutes on convention bake. Poke with fork—apples are soft when done.

4. Enjoy

Serve warm upside down (apples over biscuit) with milk or vanilla ice cream on top.

Thank You

I am grateful to Michelle and Bill for reading as writers,
Jake and Elliot for being my first editors,
Mary for pointing out my constellation,
Kris, who wanted more details,
Donna for the dung clock and decades of friendship,
Glen for staying up all night,
Christy for unfailing encouragement and
for crying in all the right places,
Jenny for making it better, and
my family, especially my brother Dave,
for sharing stories and making more.

My love to the wonderful grandmothers in my life,
especially Alma Kenyon, Genevieve Price, Dorothy Stiles,
Nanny Futia, and the real Mrs. Sackets,
who always had a quarter ready.

A special thanks to my mom,
who showed me that sometimes strength and courage
have little to do with being brave and much to do with
getting up in the morning with a little bit of faith,
and to my dad and Bob, who lived for each day
and believed.

About the Author

Karen Pavlicin grew up in upstate New York and now lives in Minnesota with her son, Alexander. They have an apple tree in their backyard and a cow dung clock in their kitchen. *Perch, Mrs. Sackets, and Crow's Nest* is her first children's novel.

Karen says, "One day I was thinking about my childhood and remembered our summertime ritual of cutting up those tiny, hard apples on Grandma's porch. For the first time I realized that it wasn't about the apples. Grandma was a smart woman—she kept her family all coming back to her porch every summer. At the same time, my son and I were beginning a new phase of our lives and I thought he could use a story about those apples. That's when I created Andy and his summer of courage."